E.G. .I.F

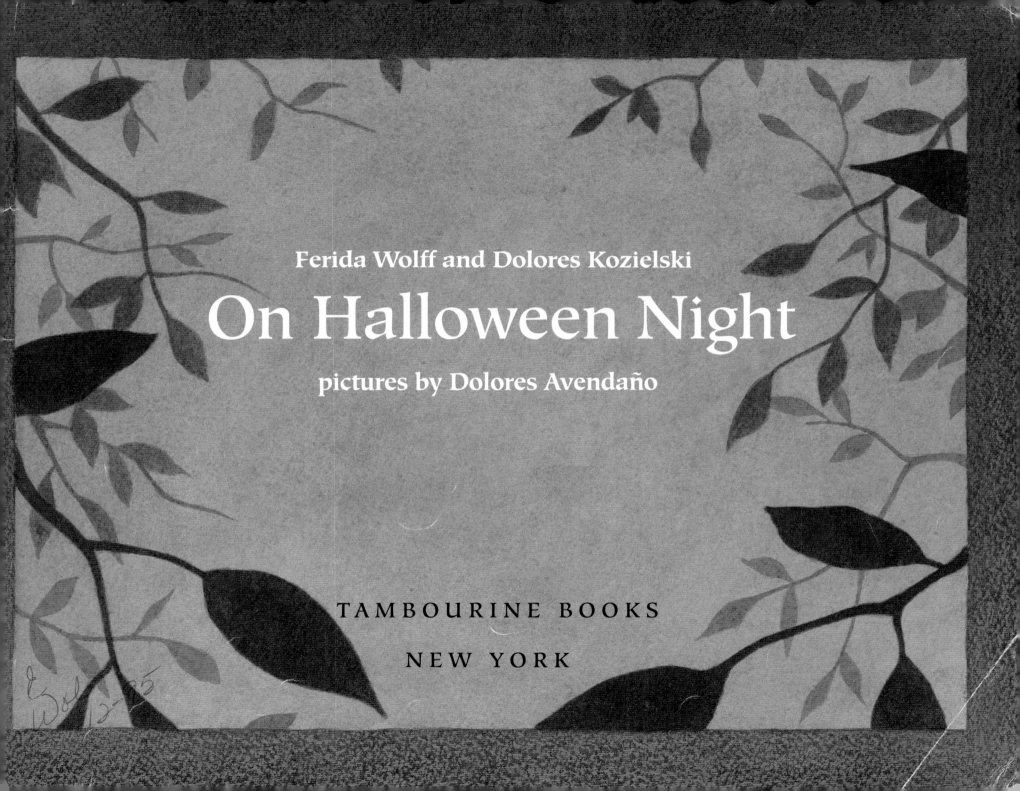

Ferida Wolff and Dolores Kozielski

On Halloween Night

pictures by Dolores Avendaño

TAMBOURINE BOOKS

NEW YORK

Books, a division of William Morrow & Company, Inc., 1350 Avenue of the
Americas, New York, New York 10019. Printed in Hong Kong by South China
Printing Company (1988) Ltd. The text type is Adobe Hiroshige.

Library of Congress Cataloging in Publication Data   Wolff, Ferida, 1946-
On Halloween night/by Ferida Wolff and Dolores Kozielski; illustrated
by Dolores Avendaño. — 1st ed. p. cm.   Summary: Thirteen suitably
creepy things from witches to snakes and ghosts are counted in
honor of Halloween. [1. Halloween—Fiction. 2. Counting.
3. Stories in rhyme.] I. Kozielski, Dolores. II. Avendaño,
Dolores, ill. III. Title. PZ8.3.W844On 1994 [E]—dc20
93-26859 CIP AC ISBN 0-688-12972-2 (TR). —
ISBN 0-688-12973-0 (LE)
10 9 8 7 6 5 4 3
First edition

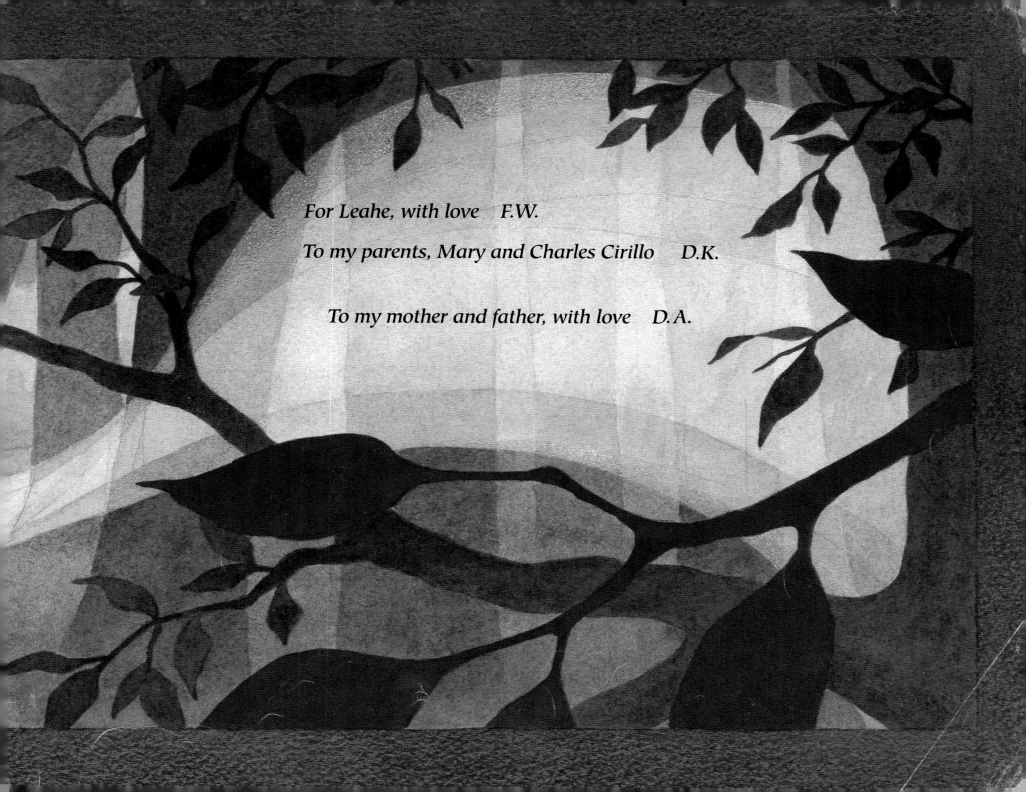

For Leahe, with love   F.W.

To my parents, Mary and Charles Cirillo   D.K.

To my mother and father, with love   D.A.

One witch stirs
up a bubbling pot,
adding this, adding that,
mixing such a tasty brew,
on Halloween night.

Oo-oo-oo-ooh.

Two cats claw
in a garbage can,
tossing this, tossing that,
digging till the morning dew,
on Halloween night.
Oo-oo-oo-ooh.

Three owls hunt
through the frosty mist,
grabbing this, grabbing that,
hooting at each startled shrew,
on Halloween night.
Oo-oo-oo-ooh.

Four goats butt
round the rattling shed,
crashing this, crashing that,
banging barn boards painted blue,
on Halloween night.
Oo-oo-oo-ooh.

Five snakes slink
over autumn leaves,
rustling this, rustling that,
sliding through an old, worn shoe,
on Halloween night.
Oo-oo-oo-ooh.

Six bears tramp
through the haunted woods,
stomping this, stomping that,
growling at the caribou,
on Halloween night.
Oo-oo-oo-ooh.

Seven wolves prowl
for a midnight meal,
stalking this, stalking that,
howling in the full moon's view,
on Halloween night.
Oo-oo-oo-ooh.

Eight toads croak
in the shivery swamp,
warning this, warning that,
hiding from a close canoe,
on Halloween night.
Oo-oo-oo-ooh.

Nine crows dance
in the pumpkin field,
flapping this, flapping that,
stamping out a tune—one, two,
on Halloween night.
Oo-oo-oo-ooh.

Ten hares hop
through the old, dried stalks,
sniffing this, sniffing that,
seeking fallen corn to chew,
on Halloween night.
Oo-oo-oo-ooh.

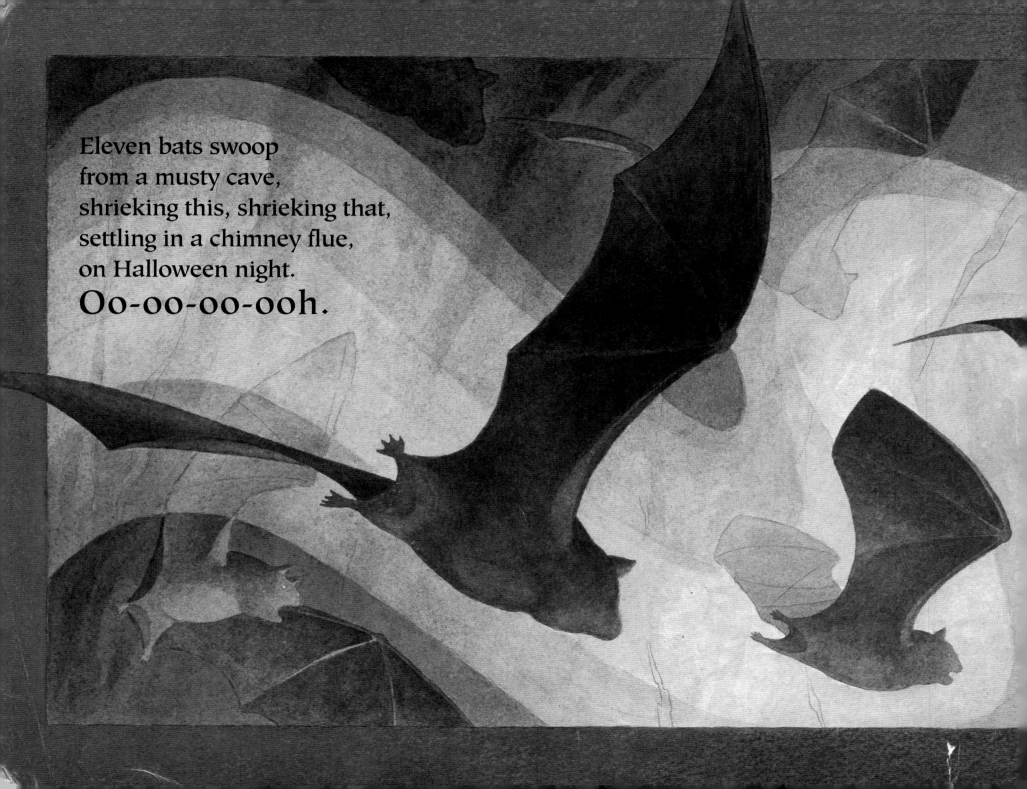

Eleven bats swoop
from a musty cave,
shrieking this, shrieking that,
settling in a chimney flue,
on Halloween night.
Oo-oo-oo-ooh.

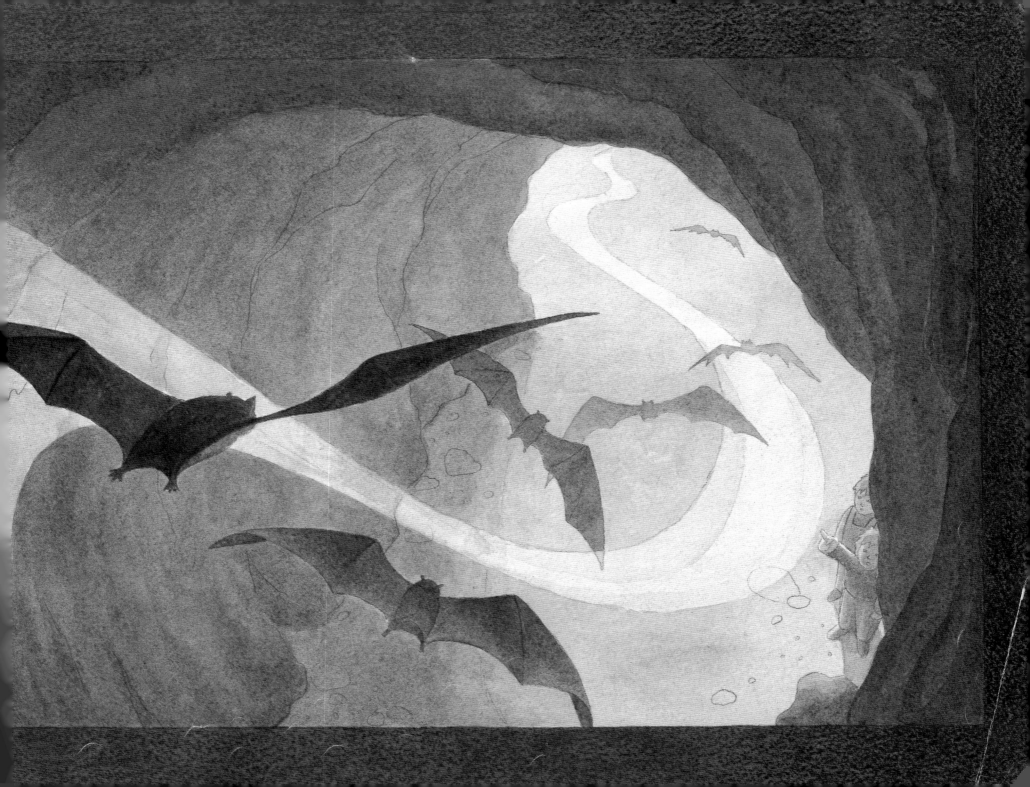

Twelve bugs creep
in a crooked house,
grubbing this, grubbing that,
feeding on cold, dried-up stew,
on Halloween night.
Oo-oo-oo-ooh.

Thirteen ghosts haunt
at the old school yard,
climbing this, climbing that,
zooming down the slide toward you,
on Halloween night.

BOOOOOO!